S0-AAZ-967

Words by Lisa Tharpe
Pictures by Ali Bahrampour

For Mira, Aiden, and Piper — LT

For Elias U. — AB

P Is For Please: A Bestiary of Manners or The ABCs Of Minding Your Ps and Qs
Text Copyright © 2009 Lisa Tharpe
Illustrations Copyright © 2009 Ali Bahrampour

All rights reserved. No part of this book may be reproduced, distributed,
or transmitted in any form or by any means, or stored in any information
distribution or retrieval system without the prior written permission of the
copyright holder except in the case of brief quotations embodied in critical
articles and reviews.

Requests for permission info@pisforplease.com

ISBN 978 – 0 – 9825320 – 1 – 0

This book was typeset in Avant Guarde Gothic BT and Lubalin Graph, Demi and Book.
The illustrations were done in pen and ink and watercolor on cold-press paper.
Designed by Denise Harris
Cover help from Robert Weinstock

Printed in Maine

First Edition
10 9 8 7 6 5 4 3 2 1

Please visit us at: www.pisforplease.com

Aa

A is for asking permission.

After eating ants with her Aunt Adele, Annie Anteater politely asks if she may be excused.

Bb

B is for brave.

Brave Bella Beaver boldly defends baby
Benjamin from bullying Boris.

Cc

C is for considerate.

Carl Cougar considerately covers his cough with the crook of his elbow to keep his germs from covering cookies, creampuffs, and other creatures.

Dd

D is for dependable.

If Damien Dingo says he's going to do the dishes or dump the trash, Daddy Dingo can count on him to do it.

Ee

E is for eating politely.

Eveline Elephant eats eagerly, but she never emits even an eek until her mouth is empty.

Ff

F is for formal.

When feasting on frog at a fancy French restaurant, Frederick Fox flaunts his finest fox manners.

Gg

G is for greetings.

Georgina Giraffe graciously greets her
gorgeous guests.

Hh

H is for helping.

Henry Hippopotamus happily helps his father
heave the heaping hamper.

Ii

I is for "I'm sorry."

"I'm sorry," says Isabella Ibis when she inadvertently injures itty bitty Iggy Iguana.

Jj

J is for "Join us!"

"Join us!" shrieks jolly Jeanie Jackrabbit when she sees Joshua Jackal joylessly juggling.

Kk

K is for kind.

When Katie Kangaroo can't think of something
kind to say, she doesn't say anything at all.

Ll

L is for listening.

Luther Lemur almost always listens to Uncle Larry's lengthy lunchtime lectures without interrupting.

Mm

M is for manners.

Mira Mongoose knows that manners are mighty. Good manners make Mamma Mongoose proud and even work their magic on mean Mr. Muskrat.

Nn

N is for "No, thank you."

"No, thank you," says Nanda Nanny Goat when her nice neighbor, Nora the Naked Mole Rat, serves fried newt and nettle noodles.

O is for open-minded.

Owen Octopus is optimistically open-minded even when it comes to trying onions, oysters, and opera.

Pp

P is for "Please."

Penelope Platypus politely pronounces "please" before petting Patrick Pig's prize-winning pet porcupine.

Qq

Q is for quiet.

Quintana Quokka knows that there are quite a few locations where, without question, one must be quiet such as libraries, lecture halls, and anywhere quokkas gather to listen to quartets.

Rr

R is for respect.

Raymond Rhinoceros respectfully treats the other animals the way he would like to be treated, even rumpled Rodney Rat.

Ss

S is for sharing.

Sofia Snake selflessly shares her special
Sunday soda with her seven serpent sisters.

Tt

T is for "Thank you."

"Thank you!" says Mrs. Tiger when tiny Timmy Tiger treats her to his tantalizing tarts.

Uu

U is for using utensils.

Umberto Uakari knows that whether he's eating udon, unagi, or Uncle Upton's famous upside-down cake, utensils are usually useful.

Vv

V is for volunteering.

Vladimir Vole valiantly volunteers to vacuum
Mrs. Vronsky's Victorian vole hole.

Ww

W is for waiting your turn.

Whether it's for watermelon, Wiener schnitzel, or Wild Willie Weasel's Waterslide, Wendell Wombat willingly waits his turn.

Xx

X is for "Excuse me!"

"Excuse me!" whispers Xavier Xolo when he accidentally bumps into an extra large xenopus.

Yy

Y is for "You're welcome."

"Thank you," says Yuri Yak. "You're welcome," yips Yolanda Yorkie. "I thought you might be yearning for a new yellow yo-yo."

Zz

Z is for zoo.

Zolinda Zorilla lives in a zoo. She
knows how to mind her manners.
How about you?